Nintendo® + ILLUMINATION

# THE SUPER MARIO BROS. MOVIE

**By Michael Moccio**

ISBN 978-0-593-64600-7 (hc)
10 9 8 7 6 5 4 3

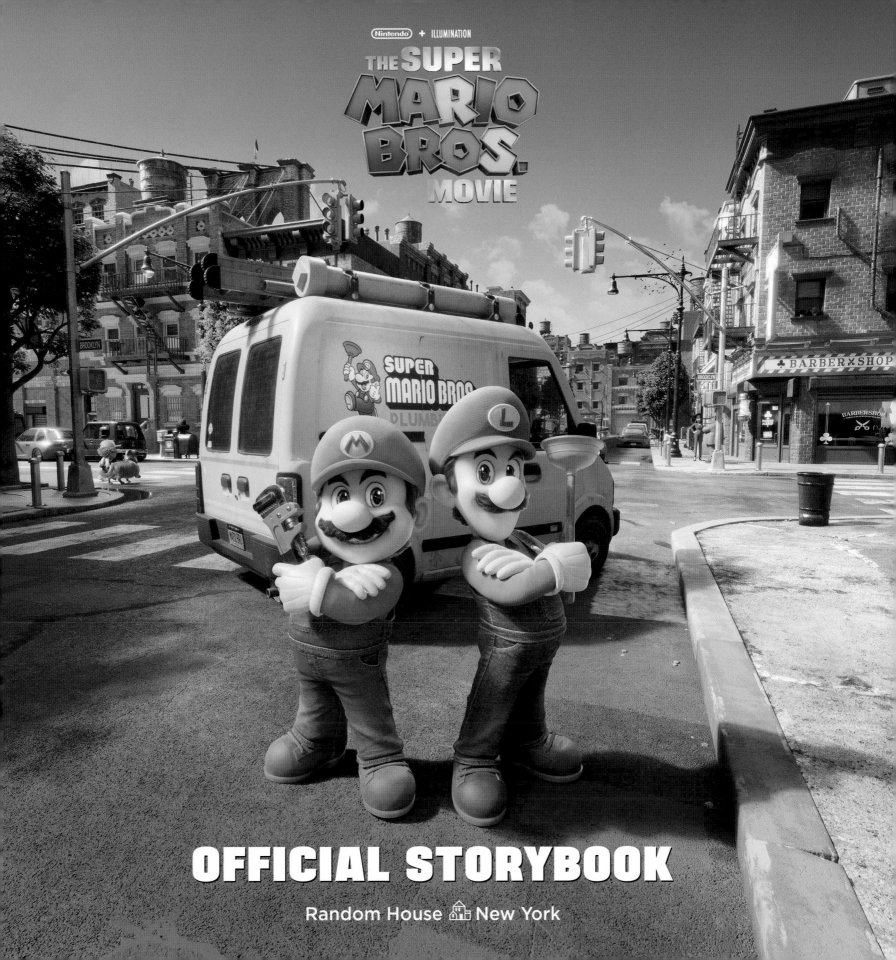

# OFFICIAL STORYBOOK

Random House 🏠 New York

# "Bowser-the King of the Koopas!"

In a fantastic world at the other end of a long pipe, trouble is brewing. And that trouble is **Bowser**, the King of the Koopas! He is obsessed with gaining power, and nothing will stop him from leading his massive army to conquer kingdoms throughout the world.

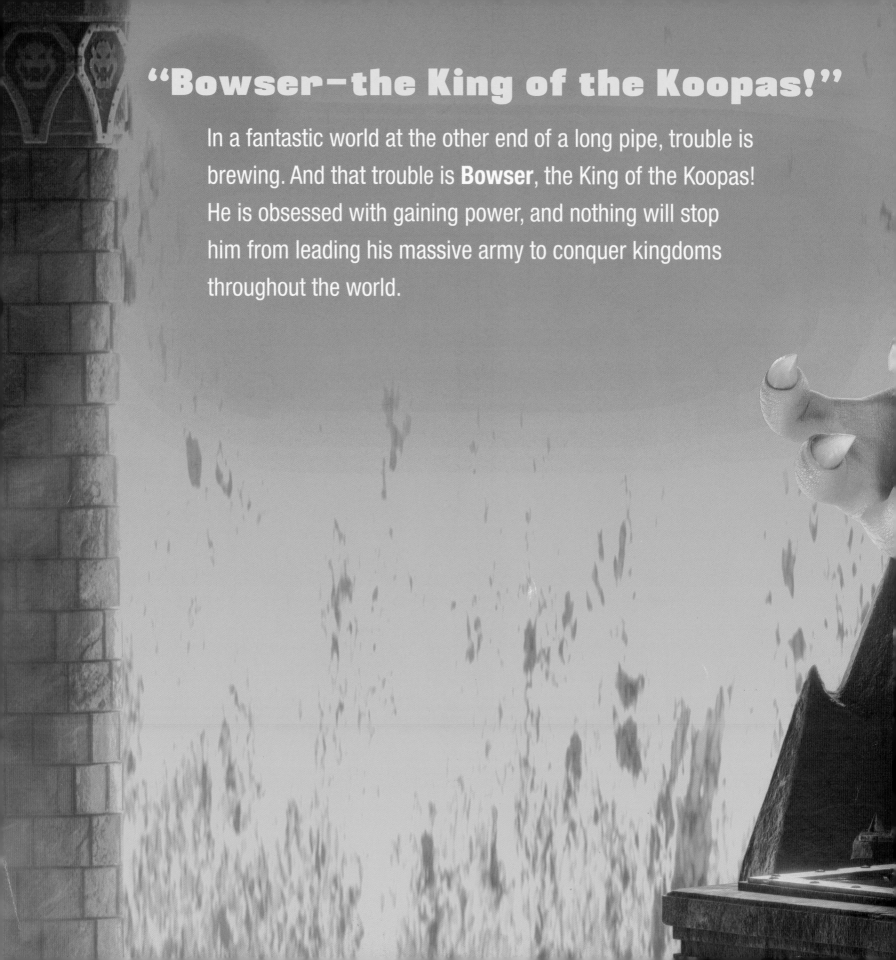

Bowser first invades the Snow Kingdom to attack the Penguin King and the Penguin Warriors at their Ice Castle. Bowser's most loyal henchman is **Kamek the Magikoopa**. He is a master of dark magic.

Kamek commands many **Koopa Troopas** who are eager to fight in Bowser's quest for power.

Though the Penguin King and the Penguin Warriors
fight fiercely with their snowballs, they're no match for
Bowser, Kamek, and the Koopa Troopas. With victory in hand,
Bowser steals the strongest Power-Up in existence: the **Super Star**.

With the Super Star, no one will be able to stop Bowser—
who now has his sights set on the Mushroom Kingdom and his
ultimate goal . . . Princess Peach.

# "We're the Mario Brothers!"

Meanwhile, in Brooklyn, New York, brothers **Mario** and **Luigi** work to make the Super Mario Bros. Plumbing Company a success. Mario's confidence and charm balance Luigi's fear and caution.

# "Let's Save Brooklyn!"

When a pipe bursts in Brooklyn, Mario and Luigi head out to save the city. Moving quickly, they go down into the sewer and are surprised to find a section of never-ending pipes. One of them pulls Mario and Luigi into a portal!

The portal separates the brothers. Mario lands alone in a mushroom forest. As Mario gets his bearings in this new world, he finds that the forest also has many, many mushrooms—his least favorite food! And Mario doesn't know it, but someone is out there watching him. . . .

# "I Am the Bravest. I Fear Nothing!"

The one who is watching Mario is **Toad**, an adorable, cheerful, and perpetually upbeat citizen of the Mushroom Kingdom! He's desperate to go on his first adventure, so when he sees Mario emerge from the pipe, he knows this is his chance!

Mario tells Toad he is looking for his brother. Toad suspects that Luigi landed in the Dark Lands, a scary place under Bowser's control. Toad says that Princess Peach, the ruler of the Mushroom Kingdom, can help Mario. He decides to bring his new friend to meet her!

# "She Can Do Anything!"

**Princess Peach** isn't your typical princess. She's strong and capable, and the sworn protector of the toads. From a young age, she has mastered Power-Ups and prepared herself to defend the Mushroom Kingdom from any threat—*even* Bowser! When Toad introduces Mario to Princess Peach, she immediately sees that Mario needs training if he hopes to help in the fight against Bowser.

But before Princess Peach can allow Mario to help, he needs to master Power-Ups. These are items that come from **Question Blocks**, which give users a wide range of special abilities. **Super Mushrooms** make you grow, while **Mini Mushrooms** make you small. Other Power-Ups, like the **Fire Flower** and **Ice Flower**, give users the ability to wield these elements. Princess Peach makes Mario run through the obstacle course again and again until he's ready.

Even with Mario's help, Princess Peach knows that Bowser and his army are just too powerful. She decides to travel to the Jungle Kingdom to convince the Kongs and their army to help. Before they go, she gives a rousing speech to the toad citizens of the Mushroom Kingdom.

Unlike Toad, who wants to go on the adventure with Mario and Peach, the other citizens of the Mushroom Kingdom tend to be very afraid. Peach's speech makes them feel a little better—but they still wish she wouldn't leave.

# "Bow Before Bowser!"

Meanwhile, Bowser and his henchman celebrate the capture of the Super Star! Kamek, all the Koopa Troopas, and other minions, party on Bowser's **airship**. Not only does Bowser use his airship to travel to and attack other kingdoms, but it also houses his prisoners. And one of those prisoners is . . .

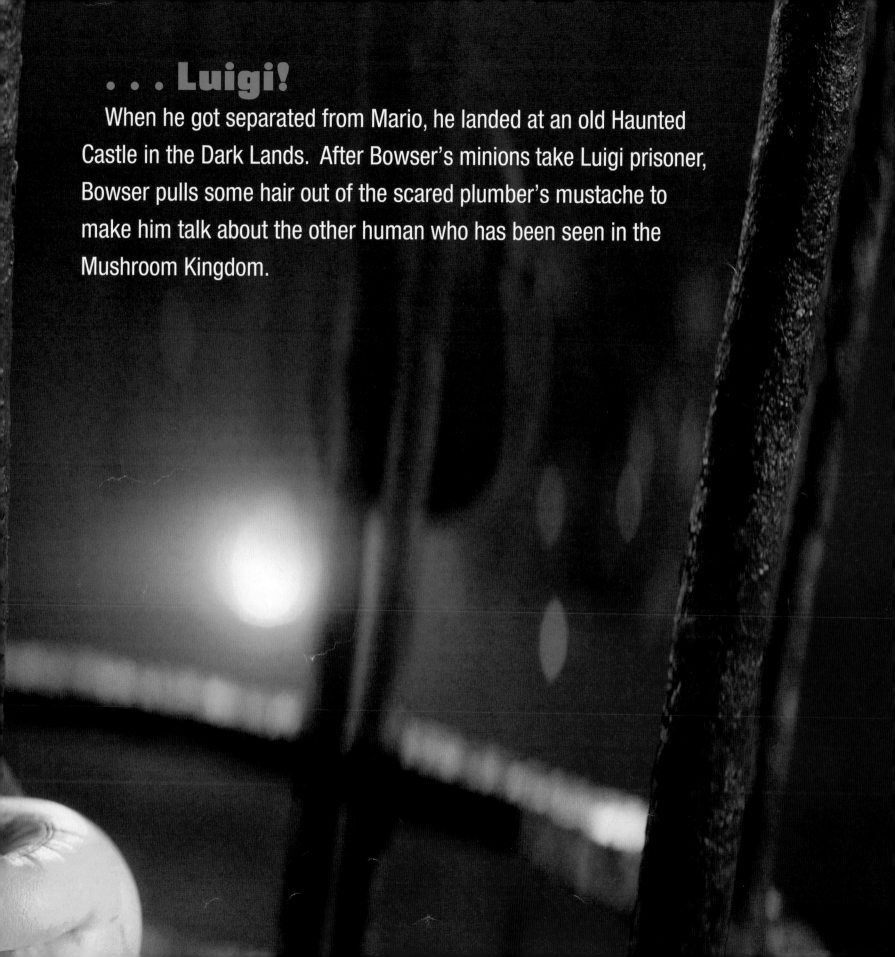

# . . . Luigi!

When he got separated from Mario, he landed at an old Haunted Castle in the Dark Lands.  After Bowser's minions take Luigi prisoner, Bowser pulls some hair out of the scared plumber's mustache to make him talk about the other human who has been seen in the Mushroom Kingdom.

Princess Peach, Mario, and Toad set off for the **Jungle Kingdom** to convince the Kong Army to fight alongside her. Perhaps together they can stand up to Bowser! When they get there, they knock politely, but will anyone let them inside?

**Cranky Kong**, the king of the Jungle Kingdom, isn't at all interested in Peach's plan, even after she reminds him that Bowser is sure to come for the Jungle Kingdom next! But when Mario speaks up, Cranky Kong tells them that if Mario can beat his son in the Great Ring of Kong, then the Jungle Kingdom will help fight Bowser and his army!

**Donkey Kong** is Cranky Kong's son and the strongest fighter in the Jungle Kingdom. Even though almost everyone, including King Cranky, dismiss Donkey Kong as someone who just loves to smash, Donkey Kong knows he has what it takes to become a great leader someday. To prove himself, he tries his best to defeat Mario.

But thanks to all the training with Princess Peach, Mario knows how to get the special Power-Ups. However, he barely defeats Donkey Kong.

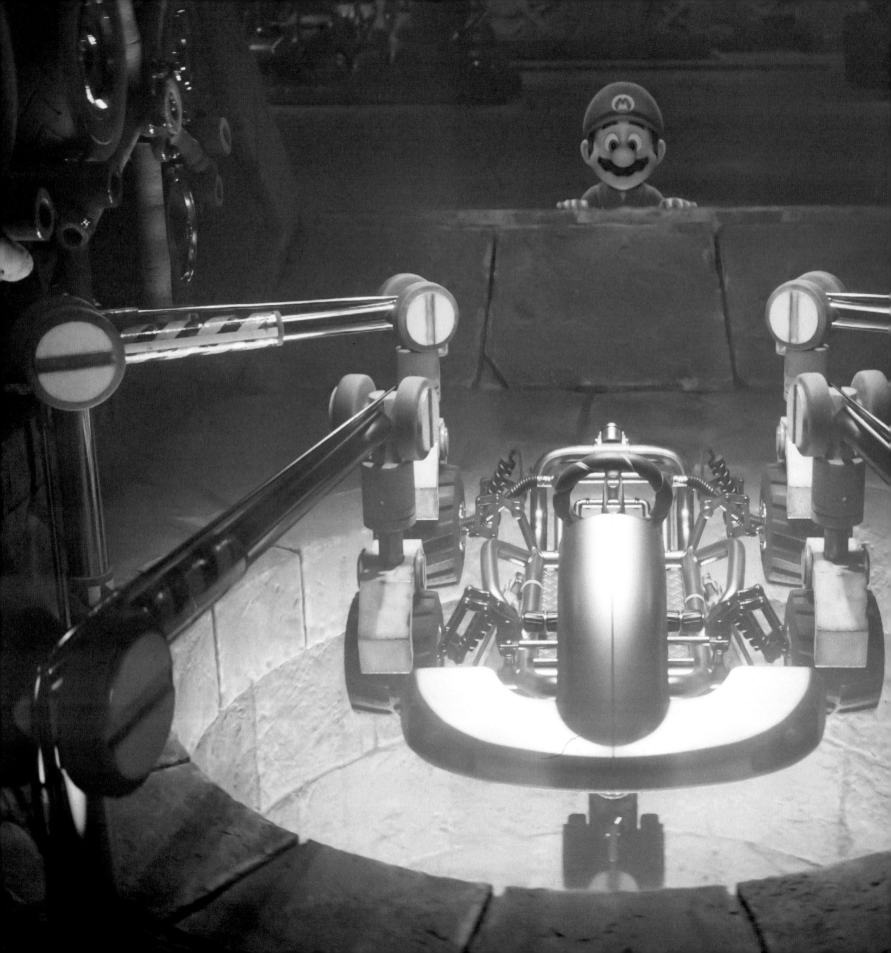

Before they can confront Bowser, Cranky Kong has Princess Peach, Mario, and Toad create their very own Karts! They'll need these fast machines if they want to catch up to Bowser's army, which has almost reached Mushroom Kingdom. Princess Peach, Mario, and Toad put their unique spin on the Kart-building process to make each vehicle their own.

## "Let's-a go!"

Now equipped with their Karts, Princess Peach, Mario, Toad, and Donkey Kong are ready to lead the Kong Army into battle against Bowser to save all the kingdoms. They must get to Bowser's army before it reaches the Mushroom Kingdom and destroys everything Princess Peach holds dear.

Their chances aren't great, but by working together, they just might
succeed in stopping Bowser!

No matter the challenge, Mario is ready to meet it! With his confidence and charm and his newfound friends and allies, Mario is ready to stand up to anything that comes his way—even Bowser!